Sun Song

Sun Song

BY JEAN MARZOLLO

ILLUSTRATED BY LAURA REGAN

HarperCollins*Publishers*

Turning, turning,
We turn toward the sun.
Each turn takes a day.
Good morning everyone.

Sun, light the woods
With a soft spring dawn;
Shine on the spots
Of a newborn fawn.

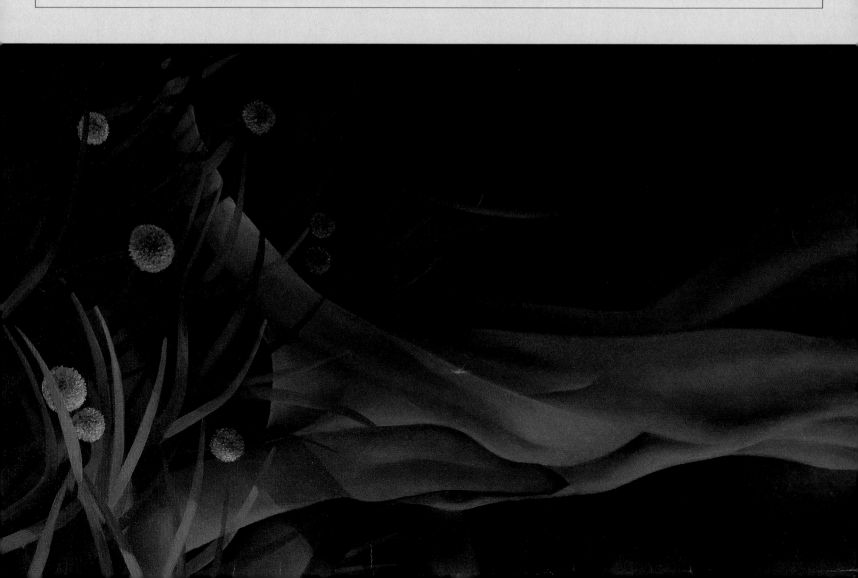

Sun, warm the rocks
At the old water hole;
Sing to the turtles
And a little brown mole.

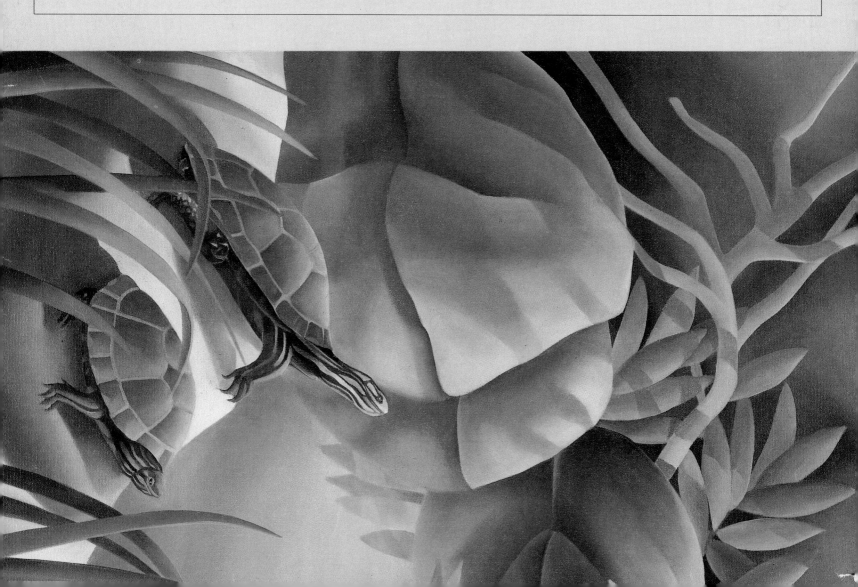

Sun, call the sheep
With the sweet scent of hay,
And warm up the nose
Of an old dappled gray.

Sun, touch the feathers
On a soft, still wing;
A blink and a bob,
And a robin starts to sing.

Sun, kiss the faces
Of a child and a pup;
With a gentle touch, tickle,
So they both wake up.

Sun, dry the dew
On the grass and the leaves,
And listen to the whisper
Of a busybody breeze.

Sun so strong,
Sun so bright,
The tulips and the lilacs
Love your light.

Sun, draw forth
The carrots and the greens;
Fill a new garden
With squash and beans.

Sun, rinse the fields
With a golden dye;
Shake out the clouds
In a wind-tossed sky.

Sun, be wild.
Sun, be bold.
Paint skies pink
And purple and gold.

Sun, slip away
From the sheep and the gray,
Munching their supper
At the end of the day.

One last peek
At the turtles and the mole,
As they settle in for night
At the old water hole.

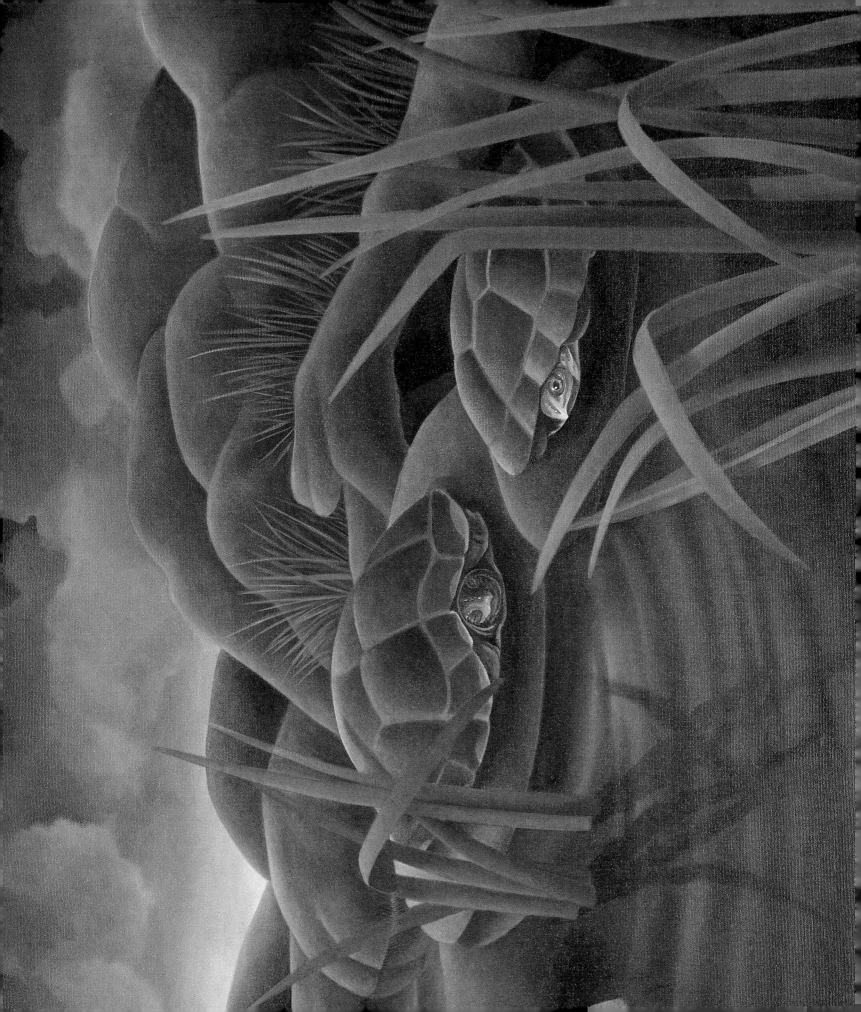

Sun, whisper, "Hush,"
To the last blue hill;
Deliver us to sleep time,
Safe and still.

Sleeping, sleeping,
We turn toward the sun
And a brand-new dawn.
Good morning, everyone.

For Patricia Adams—
and her wonderful family

—J.M.

For my stepsons Michael, Gregory, and Christopher—
who love life in the country

—L.R.

With thanks to Jim Rod, Irene O'Garden, Antonia Markiet, Al Cetta,
Willa Perlman, Molly Friedrich, Charlie Peck, Country Mouse (the puppy), and
Martha Dimock

Sun Song

Text copyright © 1995 by Jean Marzollo
Illustrations copyright © 1995 by Laura Regan
Printed in the U.S.A. All rights reserved.

Library of Congress Cataloging-in-Publication Data
Marzollo, Jean.
Sun song / by Jean Marzollo ; illustrated by Laura Regan.
    p.   cm.
Summary: Animals and plants respond to the sun's changing light over the course of
a single day.
ISBN 0-06-020787-6. — ISBN 0-06-020788-4 (lib. bdg.)
[1. Sun—Fiction.   2. Day—Fiction.   3. Stories in rhyme.]   I. Regan, Laura, ill.
II. Title.
PZ8.3.M4194Su   1995   91-29316
[E]—dc20   CIP
                                                                                  AC

Typography by Al Cetta
1 2 3 4 5 ❖ 6 7 8 9 10
First Edition